ENCHANTED

A Dream Come True

Adapted by Sarah Nathan
Based on the screenplay written by Bill Kelly
Executive Producers Chris Chase, Sunil Perkash, Ezra Swerdlow
Produced by Barry Josephson and Barry Sonnenfeld
Directed by Kevin Lima

 PRESS
New York

Printed in the United States of America
First Edition
1 3 5 7 9 10 8 6 4 2
Library of Congress Catalog Card Number: 2007901738
ISBN-13: 978-1-4231-0909-9
ISBN-10: 1-4231-0909-0

Once upon a time, there was a girl named Morgan. She lived in New York City with her dad, Robert. She believed in tales of princesses and castles and magical lands.

Her father was a busy lawyer, and he *didn't* believe in princesses. But then one night, something magical happened. A maiden arrived in Manhattan. She wandered, lost and alone, until she saw a giant billboard shaped like a castle.

Meanwhile, Morgan and her father were on their way home. Looking up, Morgan let out a gasp. She couldn't believe what she saw. It was a princess! And she was in trouble!

Robert looked up and saw the maiden. She had slipped off a billboard walkway and was dangling high above the city street.

"Catch her, Daddy!" Morgan yelled. He ran over and held out his arms just as the woman fell. But she fell from very high up, and Morgan's father was not *that* strong. With a thud, the pair landed on the ground.

Morgan rushed over to help her father and the maiden, whose name was Giselle. She was from the faraway land of Andalasia. She told them that she had fallen down a well and arrived in this strange city.

Giselle explained that she was waiting for Prince Edward to come. He was going to give her a kiss of true love. It was the most powerful thing in the world. A kiss like that could make dreams come true.

Chapter 2

Morgan convinced her father to bring
Giselle home. But when the maiden
tried to walk into their apartment, her
wide skirt got stuck in the doorway!
Morgan grabbed Giselle's hand and
gave her a strong pull.

Finally, Giselle tumbled into the apartment. "Are you really a princess?" Morgan asked when they were all inside. Giselle explained that she wasn't one . . . yet. She would have to marry Prince Edward for it to be official.

Soon after, Giselle fell asleep on the
couch. The maiden looked like a
sleeping beauty. Morgan begged her
dad to let Giselle stay. Finally, he
agreed.

The next morning, Morgan woke up to singing. It was Giselle! She had called upon a few little furry friends to help her clean the apartment. It was Giselle's way of saying thank you.

Suddenly, Morgan heard a plate crash to the floor. She opened her bedroom door and peered into the living room. Two rats scurried by her. They were on the way to do the laundry!

All over the apartment were rats,
bugs, and pigeons! They were busy
cleaning . . . and whistling while they
worked!

Morgan ran into her dad's bedroom. He was still asleep, but Morgan woke him up. "Daddy, you have to come see! Now!" Her dad was not going to believe what was happening!

When Robert walked into the living room, he got *very* angry. He asked Morgan to help him get rid of the little creatures. They picked them up by their tails and put them outside. When that was done, they took a look around. The apartment was superclean!

Before Morgan could ask Giselle how she got the animals to clean, it was time for school. While Morgan got ready, Giselle made herself a new dress. When Morgan saw it, she gasped. It was made out of the curtains from the living room!

Chapter 3

That night, Robert took Morgan
and Giselle out to dinner. They were
having a great time until a chipmunk
jumped on Giselle. But she did not get
upset. It was Pip—her friend from
Andalasia!

Later, tucked in bed, Giselle told
Morgan about Pip. He had come to
help her and to tell her Prince Edward
was in the city. When Morgan heard
that, she smiled. Giselle told the best
stories.

The next morning, Giselle made another dress. This time the material was from Morgan's bedroom curtains! Morgan did not mind—as long as Giselle stayed. But then, Prince Edward arrived.

Now that Giselle's prince had found her, Morgan and her dad had to say good-bye to the maiden. Morgan was very sad, and so was her dad. Robert liked having Giselle around, too.

Morgan missed Giselle. So that
afternoon, she put on her own
princess outfit. Looking in the mirror,
she couldn't believe her eyes. Giselle
was standing in her room!

She was going to a ball and needed a dress. But there was a problem. "I don't know where to find a fairy godmother at this late hour!" she cried. Morgan didn't hesitate. She looked at Giselle and smiled.

"I have something better than a fairy godmother!" Morgan ran out and got a credit card. "Daddy says it's only for emergencies." Morgan thought that a princess without a dress for the ball was indeed an emergency!

Chapter 4

Shopping princess-style was a ton of
fun. Morgan and Giselle went to all
the best stores in New York City.
Giselle had many bags. After all, a girl
going to a ball needs lots of things.

When they were done shopping, they went to a salon for a royal beauty treatment. They relaxed as they had their hair styled and got manicures and pedicures. "So is this what it's like going shopping with your mother?" Morgan asked.

Giselle was touched by Morgan's question. She answered honestly. "I don't know. I never went shopping with my mother."

"Me, either," Morgan said. Then she grinned at Giselle. "But I like it."

That evening, Giselle went to the ball with Prince Edward. They took a taxicab, not a pumpkin carriage. Giselle looked beautiful in her new dress. When she arrived, she saw Robert. He had come to the ball, too!

After the ball, Robert went home to tuck Morgan into bed. He told her all about the ball. He told her how Giselle saved him from a mean beast and how she finally got her true love's kiss.

And the best part? The kiss wasn't
from Prince Edward. It was from him!
Soon after, Giselle and Robert got
married and started Andalasia
Fashions, where Giselle created lots
of beautiful princess dresses for little
girls. They were made of real fabric—
not just curtains!

Being with Giselle and her dad was the best feeling in the world. Morgan could not have been happier. All her dreams had come true.